W9-BPZ-329

David Gets in Trouble

By David Shannon

THE BLUE SKY PRESS

An Imprint of Scholastic Inc. · New York

AUTHOR'S NOTE

A few years ago, my mother sent me a book I made when I was a little boy. It was illustrated with drawings of David doing all sorts of things he wasn't supposed to do, and the text consisted entirely of the words "no" and "David"—they were the only words I knew how to spell! I thought it would be fun to make a new version celebrating all the time-honored ways moms say "no." Like the original, it was called *No, David!*.

In the sequel, *David Goes to School.*, David found out that his teacher had her own ways of saying "no."

Well, now it's David's turn to speak, and it turns out that "no" is a big part of his vocabulary, too. Of course, when his mom says "no," it's because she worries about his safety, and she wants him to grow up to be a good person. Deep down, she's really saying, "I love you." But when David says "no," it usually means "I don't want to get in trouble!"

To my little troublemaker, Emma; and to Heidi, her mom, who has to say "no."

THE BLUE SKY PRESS

Copyright © 2002 by David Shannon
All rights reserved.
No part of this publication may be reproduced, or stored in a retrieval system,
or transmitted in any form or by any means, electronic, mechanical, photocopying,
recording, or otherwise, without written permission of the publisher.
For information regarding permission, please write to: Permissions Department,
Scholastic Inc., 557 Broadway, New York, New York 10012.
SCHOLASTIC, THE BLUE SKY PRESS, and associated logos are trademarks
and/or registered trademarks of Scholastic Inc.
Library of Congress catalog card number: 2001043980
ISBN 0-439-05022-7

10 9 8 7 6 5 4 3 2 1   02 03 04 05 06
Printed in Mexico   49
First printing, September 2002

When David gets in trouble,
he always says . . .

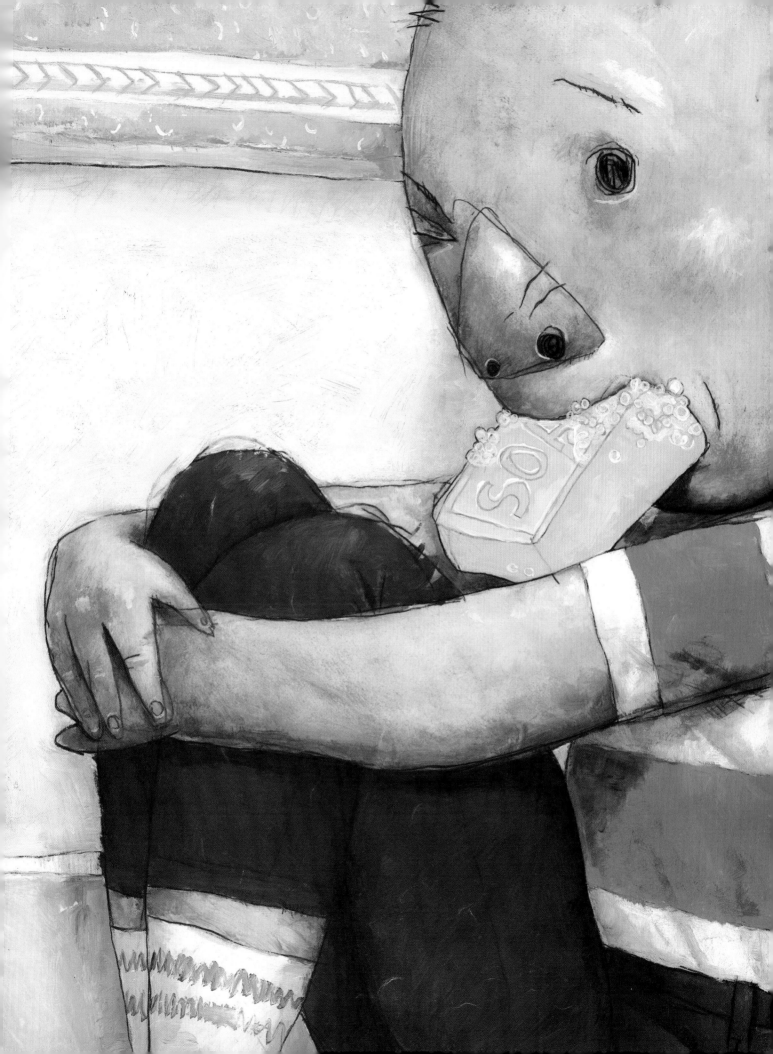

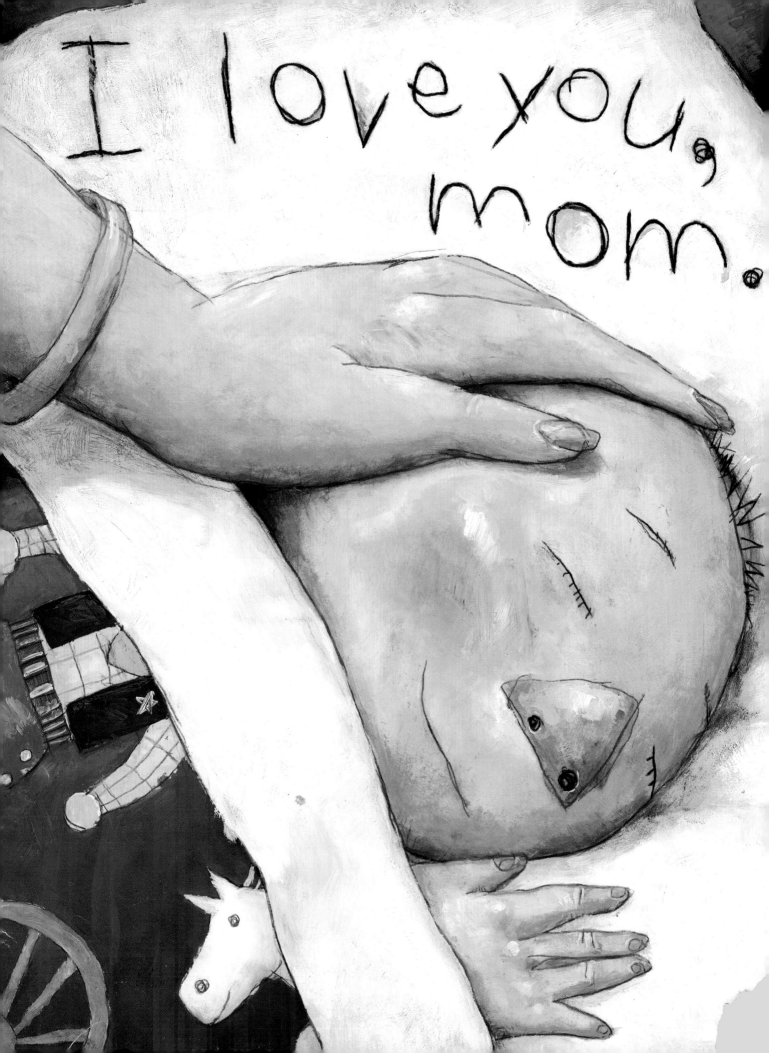